WHEN
THE PORCUPINE
MOVED IN

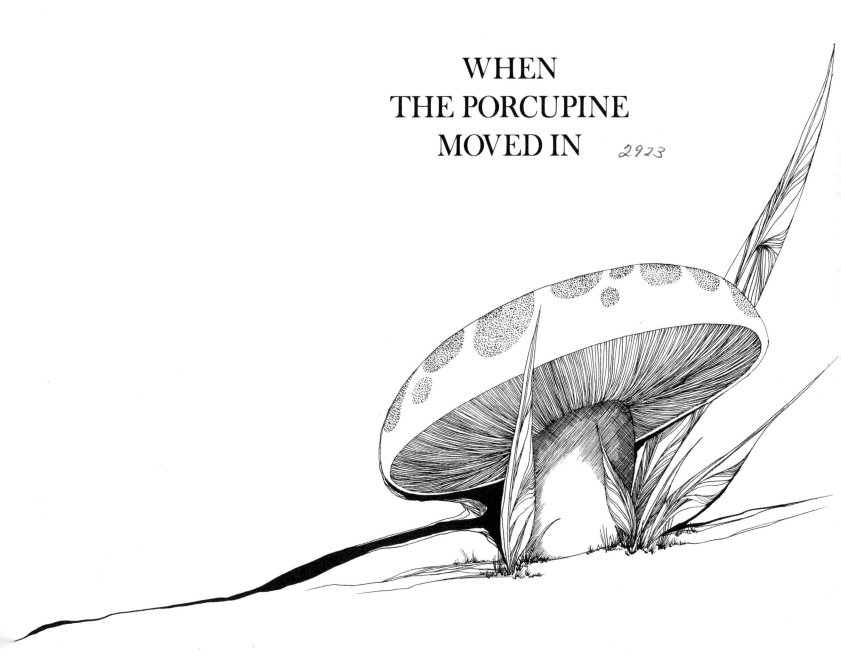

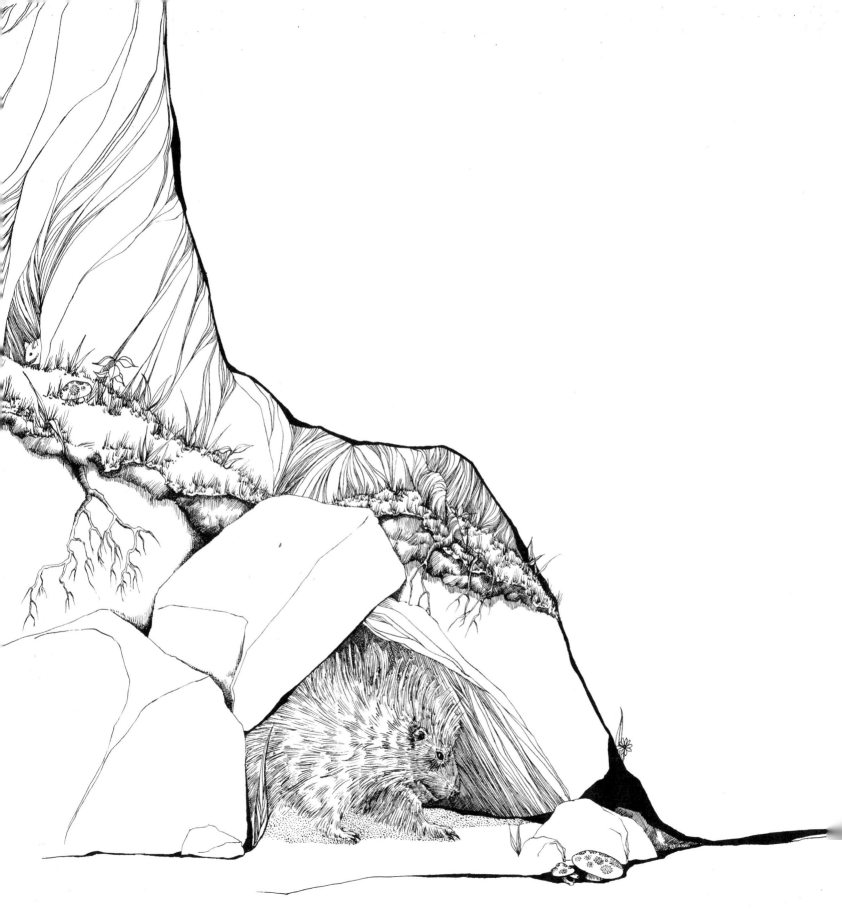

WHEN THE PORCUPINE MOVED IN

BY CORA ANNETT
ILLUSTRATED BY PETER PARNALL

Franklin Watts, Inc.
845 Third Avenue
New York, N.Y. 10022

SBN 531-01987-x
Library of Congress Catalog Card Number: 71-131152

3 4 5 6 7 8 9 10

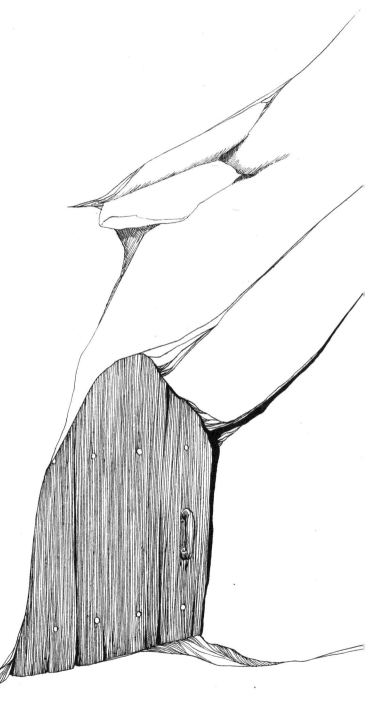

One day in early autumn when the wind was brisk, the Porcupine went to visit the Rabbit.

He sat at the Rabbit's kitchen table, gazing thoughtfully at the bright clean curtains and at the glowing fire burning cozily in the fireplace to take the damp morning chill from the air.

Then he said to the Rabbit, "You and I are good friends. In fact, we are such good friends that I have decided to move in with you in order to keep you from getting lonely on long winter nights. We shall tell each other stories and warm our toes at the fire and it will work out very nicely because good friends always get along perfectly together and we are *very* good friends."

(He did not mention that his own house was damp and drafty and badly in need of repair, and that it was much more agreeable to move out of it than to think of fixing it up.)

The Rabbit did not think they were quite so friendly as all that, but what could he do? It was difficult to disagree with the Porcupine, for if you did he would get angry and shout. What was even more alarming, he would grow bristly all over. It was better to hold your tongue and wait for him to change his mind all by himself—which he almost never did.

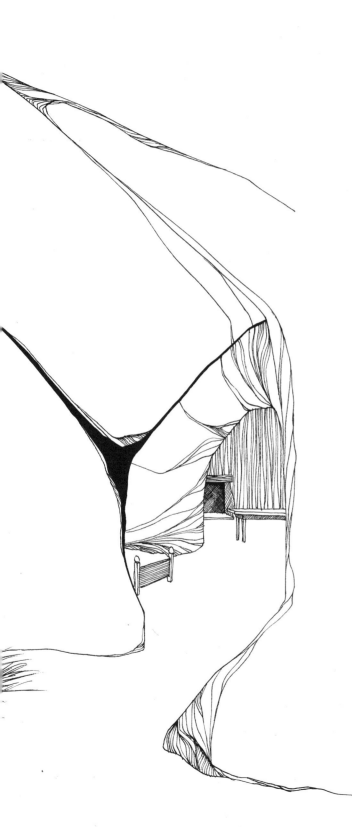

He certainly did not change his mind about moving in with the Rabbit. The next afternoon he carried all his belongings over and put them away in the Rabbit's drawers and cupboards. Then he took the Rabbit's bed to sleep in, so that the Rabbit had to fix up a cot for himself in a corner of the kitchen. Then he sat down in the Rabbit's favorite chair next to the fireplace, so that the Rabbit was forced to sit on the footstool.

Then he smiled with satisfaction and said, "I think we'll get along just fine together."

And since the Rabbit was an easygoing, good-natured sort, it seemed likely that they would. At least, it seemed that way right in the beginning. That same evening, things began to look a bit different.

The Rabbit said, "It's time for supper. I will get it ready."

"What are we having?" asked the Porcupine.

"I am going to make a fine salad with lettuce and carrots and cucumbers and radishes and cabbage," said the Rabbit.

"I don't like salad," the Porcupine said firmly. "We will have beans and brown bread instead."

And so they ate beans, even though the Rabbit always got an upset stomach from eating them, and he had the hiccups all the rest of the evening until bedtime.

The next morning when they got up it was raining.

"This will be a good day to clean house," said the Rabbit.

"Nonsense!" said the Porcupine. "We will do the gardening, instead."

"But—but it's raining," said the Rabbit.

"So? What's a little rain? You are much too finicky, my friend," answered the Porcupine.

And they went out in the rain and did the gardening. They got soaked through and through and the Rabbit had to go to bed early that night with the sniffles.

The next day the sun was shining brightly.

"What a fine day to go down to the pond and catch some fish for our supper!" said the Rabbit.

"Today we will clean house," the Porcupine said flatly. "We still have some leftover beans for supper."

So they cleaned house and never got to go out in the sunshine at all. That evening the Rabbit had the hiccups again from eating beans for supper, and a headache besides from being very annoyed and not daring to say so.

Slowly he was beginning to realize something else about his friend. It was not only difficult to disagree with the Porcupine. It was also impossible for the Porcupine *not* to disagree with *you*. No matter what you might say, he was sure to be contrary about it and do just the opposite.

If the Rabbit went to open the window, the Porcupine would exclaim, "No, no! I can't stand the draft. I'll be dead of pneumonia within the week."

If the Rabbit went to close the window, the Porcupine would gasp, "Air! I need fresh air!"

If the Rabbit started to make a fire in the fireplace, the Porcupine said they must not be wasteful with the firewood.

If the Rabbit thought it was too warm for a fire, the Porcupine accused him of being stingy with the firewood.

But the Rabbit was a good-natured, easygoing sort, and they managed to live together without any quarrels throughout the autumn and into the winter.

At Christmas the Rabbit always went to visit his relatives. He looked forward eagerly to going, for they would have a large gathering with lots of delicious things to eat and much singing and merriment that would last far into the night. On Christmas morning he politely invited the Porcupine to come along with him.

But the Porcupine had gotten up in a bad mood and looked even more stubborn than usual. He thought for a moment, as if he were trying to find the most contrary thing he could think of to say. At last he replied, "I want to go fishing."

"Fishing!" said the Rabbit. "In the middle of winter? Why, the pond is frozen over."

"Nevertheless, I want to go fishing," said the Porcupine. "And you must come with me, for it would not be right for you to leave your guest— that's me—all alone at Christmas."

There was nothing for the Rabbit to do but go fishing with the Porcupine. They gathered together their fishing rods and baskets, and they bundled up in heavy coats and went shivering down to the pond.

They had to break a hole in the ice, shaking their paws from time to time and blowing on them to keep them from freezing. Then they sat holding

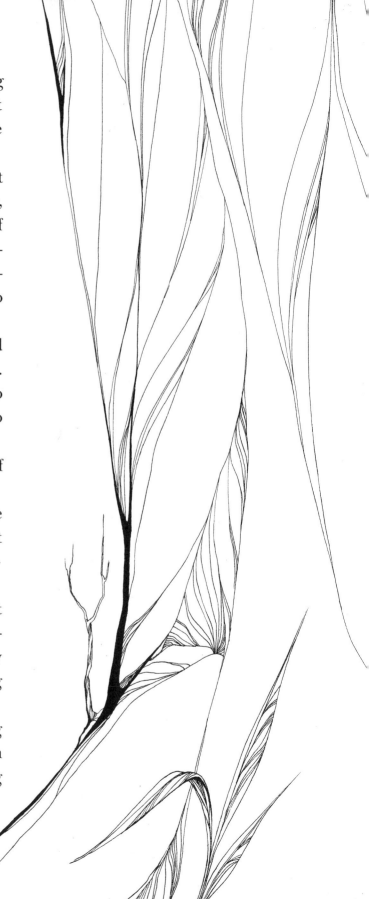

their fishing rods, with their noses buried in their scarves and their teeth chattering and their whole bodies shaking with cold.

They sat there all day, and in the end they had caught nothing. The only thing the Rabbit managed to do was to get his hook stuck on something under the water. He had to creep out on the ice to try to pull it free. He got it loose, but just as he did so the ice cracked under him and down he went—*sploosh!*—into the icy water.

"Help!" he gurgled.

The Porcupine began running back and forth along the bank, wringing his paws and looking awfully upset. "Are you drowning?" he cried. "Oh, you aren't drowning, are you?"

"No, I'm not drowning," the Rabbit answered. "I am *freezing* to death. And if you don't get me out of here at once, you'll have no one to disagree with any more."

The Porcupine crept gingerly out onto the ice and fished the Rabbit out. Then they got their things together and went home. By the time they got there the Rabbit had icicles hanging from his nose and ears and paws, and was shaking so hard he could not talk.

After all that, they still had no fish for their supper. But fortunately the Porcupine found some beans in the cupboard. The Rabbit took one look at them and went straight to bed with chills and fever.

The next morning he woke up with a terrible cold. For three days he lay in bed, shivering and coughing and sneezing. During that time the Porcupine took care of him, bringing him his meals in bed, and even reading him stories. He was as sweet and agreeable as could be, for he was somewhat ashamed of himself for having been the cause of it all. In fact, he was so very good that the Rabbit was sure he had reformed. But no sooner was the Rabbit better than the Porcupine became himself again and acted even more contrary than ever, if that were possible, to make up for lost time.

And so they continued in the same way as before, throughout the winter and into the spring.

Every year, in springtime, all the animals for miles around gathered together and had a grand picnic to celebrate the new season. There were always lots of delicious things to eat. There were footraces and other games, with prizes for the winners. And in the evening the animals toasted marshmallows over a bonfire and sang songs far into the night. *Everyone* would be there.

The Rabbit wanted very much to go, but he did not know how he was going to get the Porcupine to agree to it. He thought and thought about it, and at last he said, as though it really didn't matter at all, "I suppose the picnic will be lots of fun this year."

The Porcupine frowned. "*What* picnic?"

"Why, you know. The picnic the animals have every year, with songs and games and toasted marshmallows"—the Rabbit could not help getting excited as he talked about it, though he tried hard not to, and his eyes grew bright as the words tumbled out faster and faster—"and strawberry pies and chocolate cake and watermelon and footraces and prizes and bonfires and *every*thing!"

Already the Porcupine's face was getting that

stubborn look on it, and the Rabbit's heart sank.

"It's a pity we can't go," said the Porcupine, but he did not really sound sorry.

"Why can't we go?" asked the Rabbit.

"Because all my relatives are coming over that day, that's why."

"But I didn't know they were coming."

"That's because I just decided to invite them, this minute."

The Rabbit's ears drooped in disappointment. Then he had a thought.

"I know," he said brightly. "*You* stay home and entertain your relatives while *I* go to the picnic."

But at that the Porcupine scowled even more fiercely, and his quills bristled up threateningly all over his body.

"*What!*" he cried. "And leave me alone to do all the work? Is that the sort of friend you are? This is your house, you know, and you must be home when guests come to visit."

The poor Rabbit did not dare say another word. There was nothing to do but stay home and entertain the Porcupine's relatives, while everyone in the whole world went to the spring picnic.

The Rabbit did not know the Porcupine had
so many relatives. When they came they filled the
house. There were porcupines sitting on all the
living-room chairs and on the sofa, and on the
kitchen chairs and on the beds. There were porcupines sitting on the windowsills and there were
porcupines sitting on the floor. There was hardly
any room for the Rabbit.

He did not know that porcupines had such good appetites, either. They ate everything in the cupboards. When they finished that, they went down into the cellar and ate all the pickled cabbage and carrots and cucumbers that the Rabbit had put up in jars and stored away. And when *that* was all gone, they went out into the Rabbit's garden and dug up almost all the new cabbages and carrots and lettuce and cucumbers and radishes, even though it was only spring and they had hardly had time yet to grow.

The Rabbit also did not know that the Porcupine's relatives were such wonderful talkers, but he soon found out. Each one of them insisted on telling his life history, without leaving out the tiniest detail. This greatly amused all the other porcupines, but it bored the Rabbit to tears. Since there were so many of the porcupines, they could not possibly get finished with all the histories in one day. So the party lasted three days.

The Rabbit was in despair. There was no corner of his house he could hide in without finding porcupines there. He could not lie down on his cot, for eight little porcupines had been put to bed in it by their mothers. There was nothing left to eat. And, what was worse than anything else, every minute he had to listen to one porcupine or another droning, "When I was a young lad—"

At last he could stand it no longer. In the wee hours of the morning on the third day, while some porcupines were still talking and others were nodding drowsily, he stole silently from the house.

He made his way down to the pond, where he sat on the bank and stared gloomily at the water. He thought about the old days, many months ago, when his little home had been his own, and his thoughts and ideas had been his own, too. He thought how nice it would be if things could be like that again.

The Rabbit thought about how contrary and stubborn and balky the Porcupine was, and how terrible the situation was, and how something simply had to be done about it right this minute.

And he sat and sat and thought and thought until he hardly saw anything around him any more, and it seemed as if a little wind nestled close to him and blew an idea into his ear.

And presently he arose and returned home. But the look in his eye was very much different from what it had been when he left. There was something a bit sly in it, you might say. There was a gleam and a glimmer in it, and there were little turned-up hooks at the corners of his mouth.

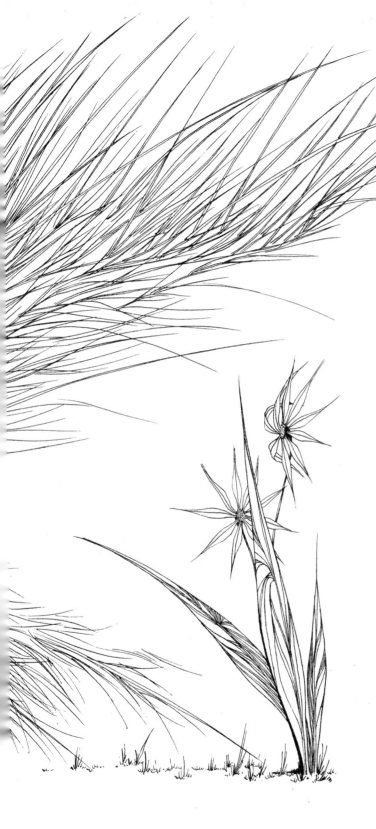

When he got home he found the Porcupine sprawled on the living-room chair, looking exhausted. All the relatives had gone.

"That was a very nice party," said the Rabbit. "We must have your relatives over again real soon."

The Porcupine looked somewhat surprised at this. It was a moment before he could answer.

"Why, it was *not*," he said at last. "It was not a nice party. It was a very dull party, and I won't have my relatives over any more."

And the Rabbit smiled to himself, but if you had not been looking very closely at the corners of his mouth, you would never have known that he smiled.

That afternoon the Rabbit said, "I would like very much to have beans and brown bread for supper."

"That's too bad," the Porcupine snapped, "because we are going to have a salad of lettuce and carrots and cucumbers and radishes and cabbage." And he went out into the garden and worked very hard trying to find some vegetables that his relatives had not dug up.

In the evening it was a bit chilly. "Well, we can't have a fire tonight," the Rabbit said, "for we must not be wasteful with the firewood."

"Nonsense!" the Porcupine retorted. "What kind of a home is it, if you can't be warm and cozy in it?" He proceeded at once to make a big fire.

And the Rabbit sat happily in his favorite chair next to the fireplace, nodding and dozing and toasting his toes.

When it was time to go to bed he yawned and stretched and said, "I'm so glad you took the bed for yourself. If it hadn't been for that, I'd never have discovered how comfortable the cot is. I shall sleep in it always."

At that the Porcupine frowned, and bit his paw. "Is that so?" he said. "Well, I have decided that I am going to sleep in it from now on. What a fine way to treat your guest—keeping the most comfortable bed for yourself!"

And the Rabbit went to sleep in his own bed for the first time in months, and in the darkness he *really* smiled.

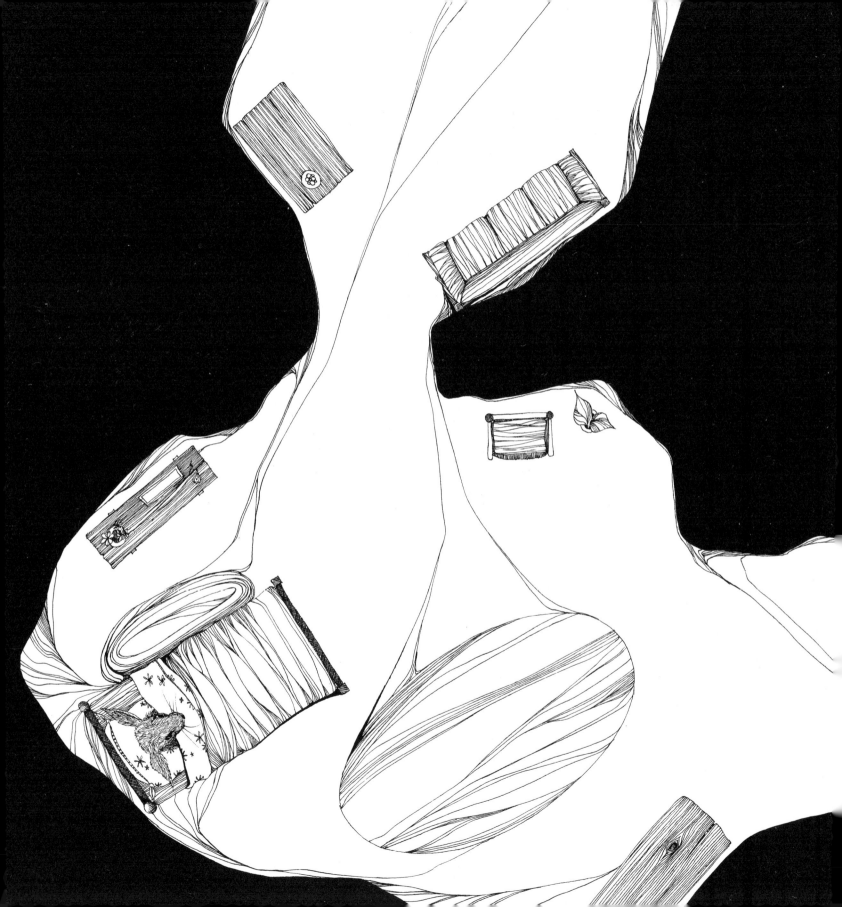

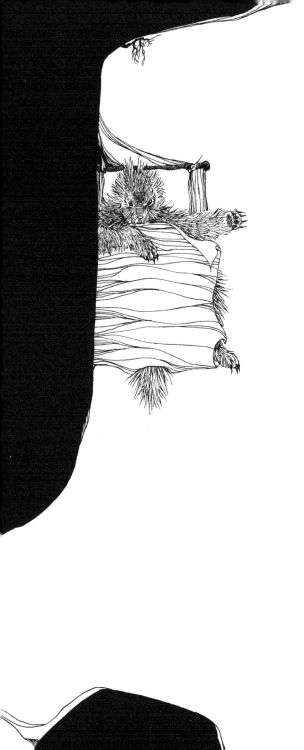

After a little bit he called out to the Porcupine, "It's so nice having you live here in my little house with me. You must stay forever and ever."

There was a long silence.

At last the Porcupine called back in a strained voice, from his cot in the kitchen, "How perfectly silly you are! Why *should* I go on living here forever? How dull that would be. In fact, I was just thinking about moving."

"Not really!" said the Rabbit. "Well, if you must, you must. But anyway, there's no hurry about it. You must stay a few more days, at least."

"And why must I, may I ask?" the Porcupine retorted. "I shall leave when I please. In fact, I'm going to move out first thing in the morning."

At that the Rabbit not only smiled—he positively grinned. And he fell asleep grinning like that.

The next morning, right after breakfast, the Porcupine packed up his belongings and moved out, though the Rabbit kept protesting all the while that he should stay.

As the Porcupine carried his things away the Rabbit stood in the doorway of his house and called after him, "Good-bye! Good-bye! I'm sorry you're going. But surely you'll change your mind and come back."

"I will not!" shouted the Porcupine crossly. "I never change my mind about anything. And I am *never* coming back!" And away he marched.

The Rabbit went inside the little house that was his again, all his, and he closed the door behind him. Then he not only smiled, he not only grinned—he laughed and laughed. He laughed all that day and far into the next. He could hardly eat his supper for laughing.

Even after he had stopped laughing over it, for years afterward he could not keep from breaking into a fit of giggling whenever he thought about it. Everyone who knew him said that he had certainly become the merriest Rabbit that anyone had ever seen or heard of.

But whenever he met up with the Porcupine
he was always polite and very careful not to smile
in the least bit, and they remained friends in spite
of everything.

Cora Annett grew up in Boston and still lives in Massachusetts. She says: "I have wanted to write ever since I was seven or eight, and in fact did write at that age—poems, a play or two, and the first three chapters of a novel (whose heroines were also seven or eight). I always loved reading, but never could find enough of the kind of books I liked best—humorous and fanciful ones. I think that is one of my motives for writing children's books now." She is the author of two other books for children: *The Dog Who Thought He Was a Boy* and *Homerhenry*.

Peter Parnall was born in Syracuse, New York, and attended Cornell University and Pratt Institute. He has illustrated many books for children, among them *A Dog's Book of Bugs, Malachi Mudge,* and *A Beastly Circus.* He and his wife and son live in New Jersey.